Alphabet Hanawriting

PRACTICE WORKBOOK

Aa   Bb   Cc

Aa   Bb   Cc

Get free additional resources to use at home or in school!

SCAN ME

SiohanPress.com

ISBN 978-1-959451-96-9
Siohan Press

_____

Write your name above.

Let's get started!

Trace the uppercase letters

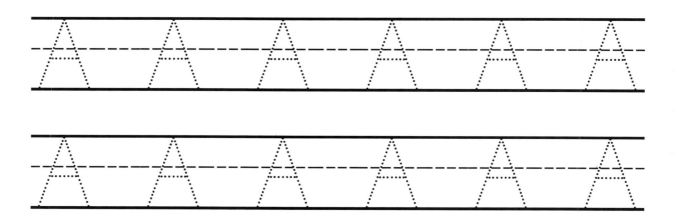

Trace the lowercase letters

Trace the uppercase letters

BBBBBB

BBBBBB

Trace the lowercase letters

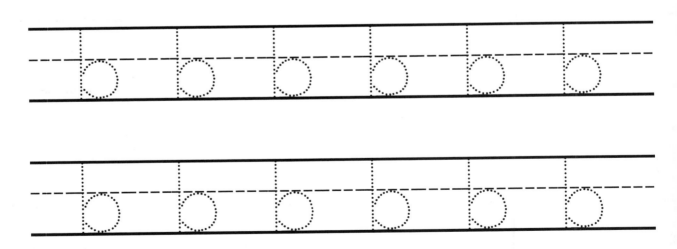

Bb

Trace the uppercase letters

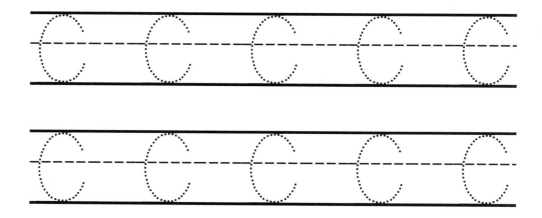

Trace the lowercase letters

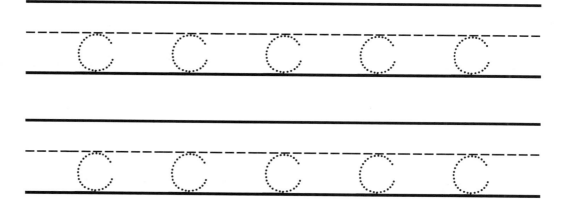

Trace the uppercase letters

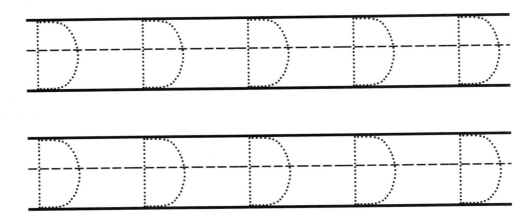

Trace the lowercase letters

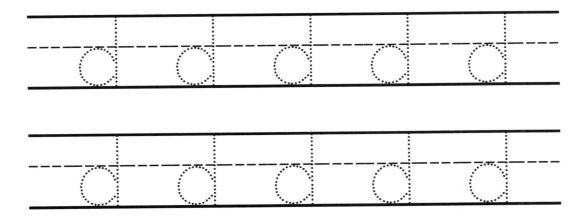

Dd

Trace the uppercase letters

Trace the lowercase letters

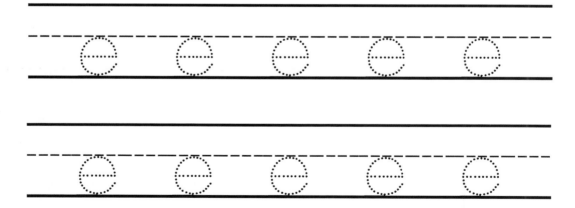

Ee

Trace the uppercase letters

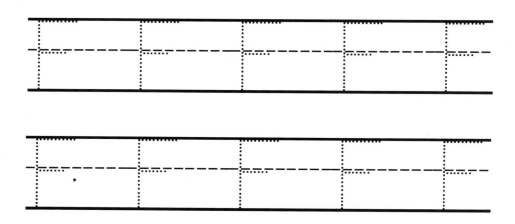

Trace the lowercase letters

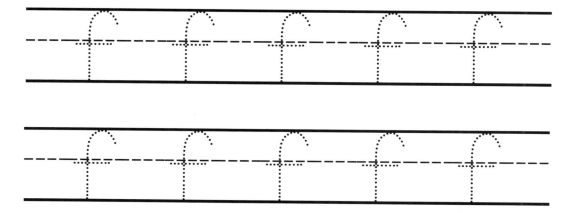

Ff

Trace the uppercase letters

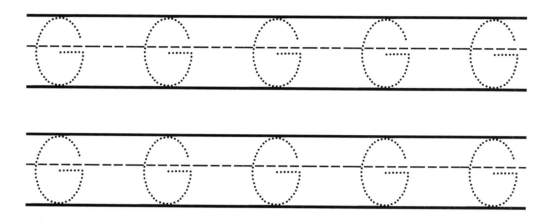

Trace the lowercase letters

Trace the uppercase letters

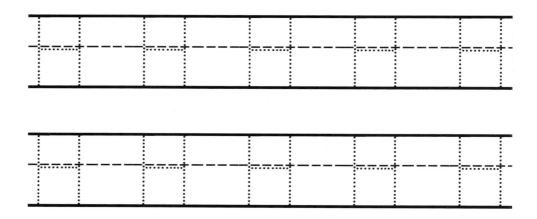

Trace the lowercase letters

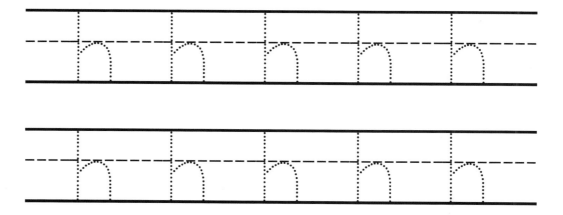

Trace the uppercase letters

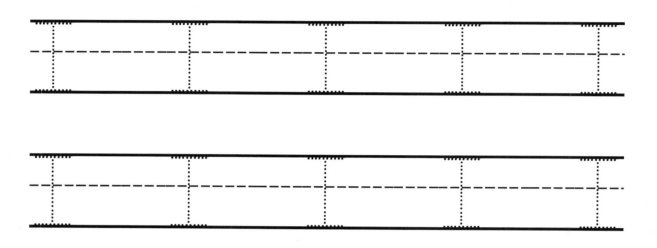

Trace the lowercase letters

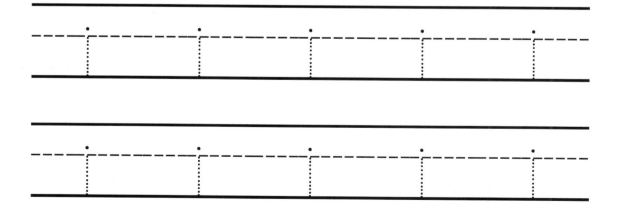

Ii

Trace the uppercase letters

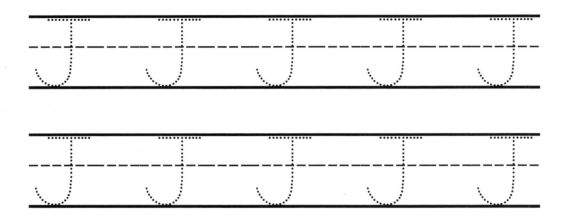

Trace the lowercase letters

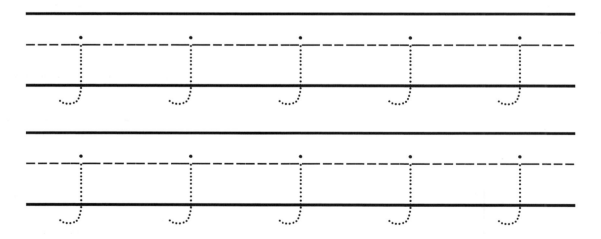

Jj

Trace the uppercase letters

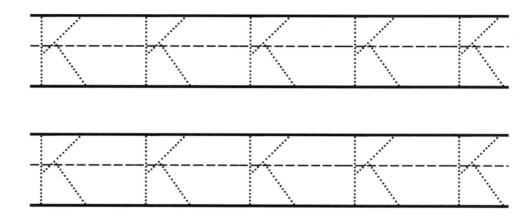

Trace the lowercase letters

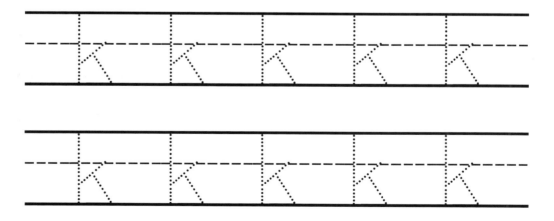

Kk

Trace the uppercase letters

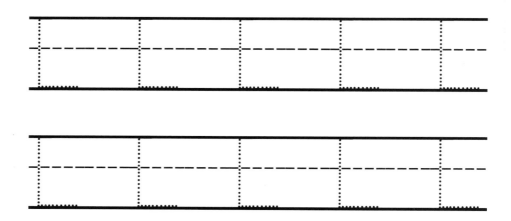

Trace the lowercase letters

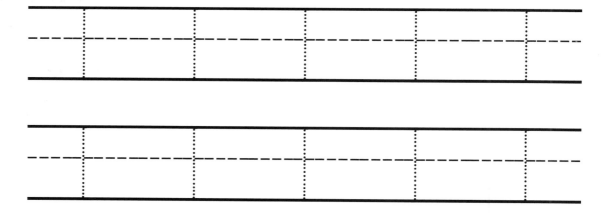

Trace the uppercase letters

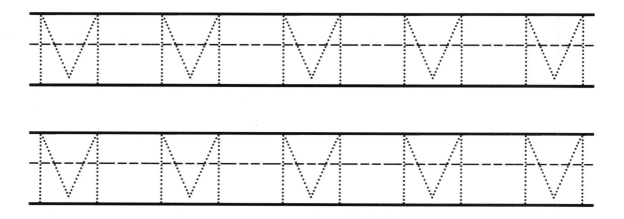

Trace the lowercase letters

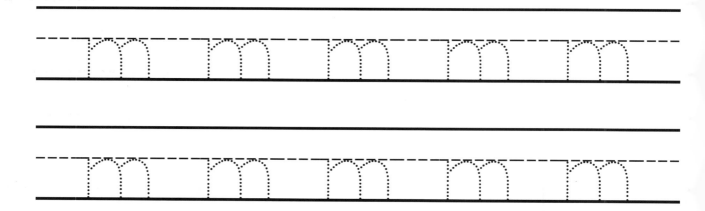

Mm

Trace the uppercase letters

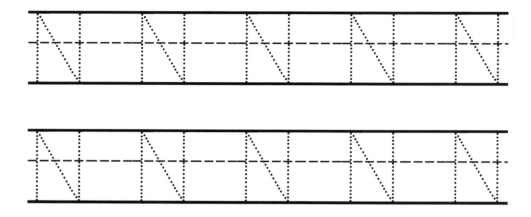

Trace the lowercase letters

Trace the uppercase letters

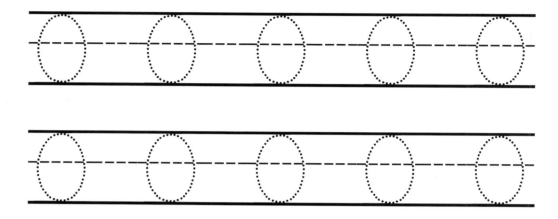

Trace the lowercase letters

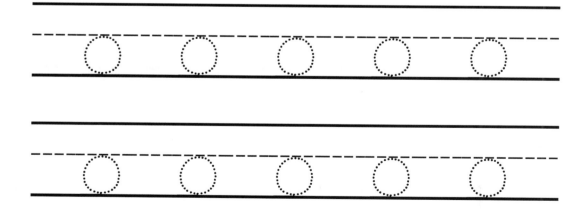

Trace the uppercase letters

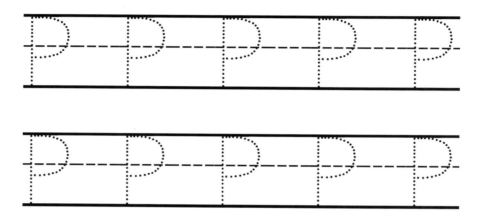

Trace the lowercase letters

Pp

Trace the uppercase letters

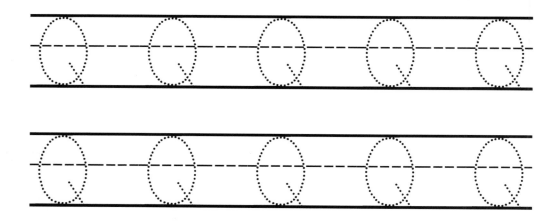

Trace the lowercase letters

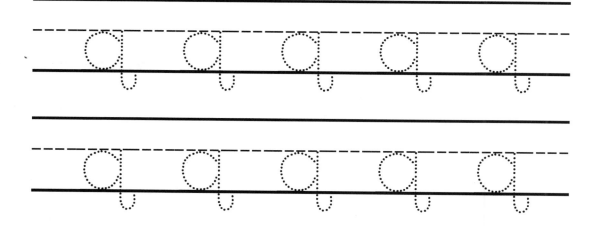

Qq

Trace the uppercase letters

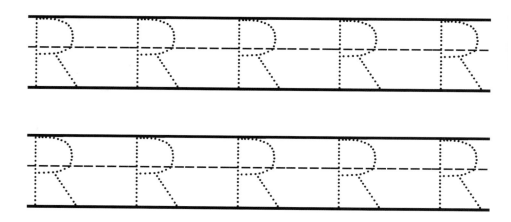

Trace the lowercase letters

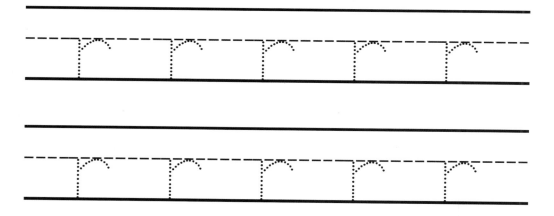

Rr

Trace the uppercase letters

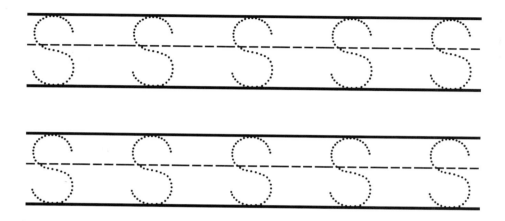

Trace the lowercase letters

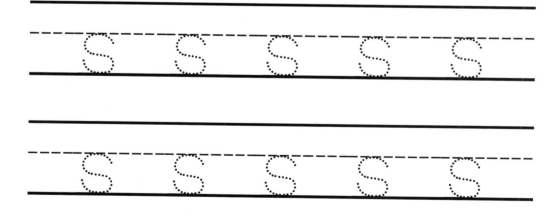

Ss

Trace the uppercase letters

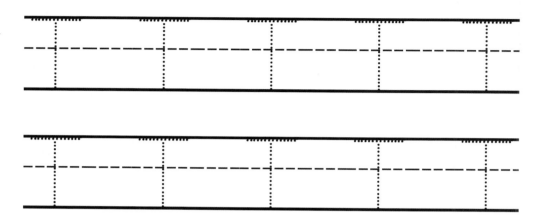

Trace the lowercase letters

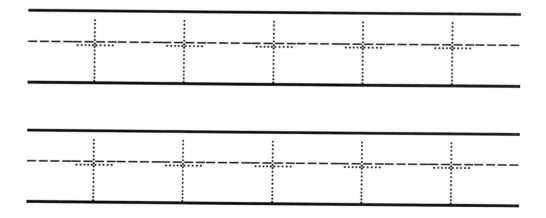

Trace the uppercase letters

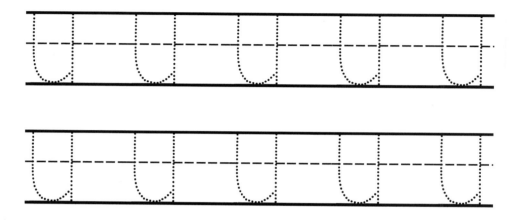

Trace the lowercase letters

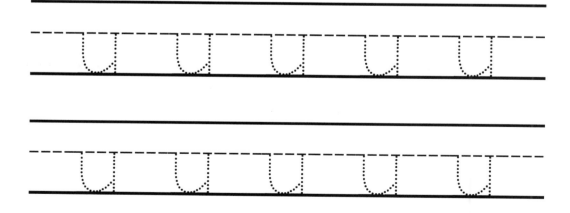

Trace the uppercase letters

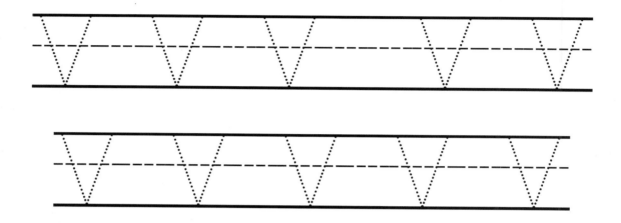

Trace the lowercase letters

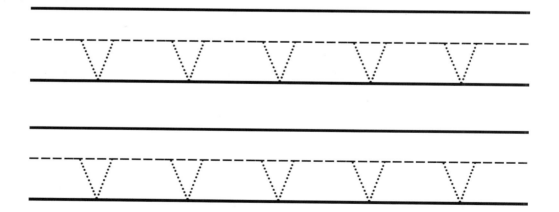

Vv

Trace the uppercase letters

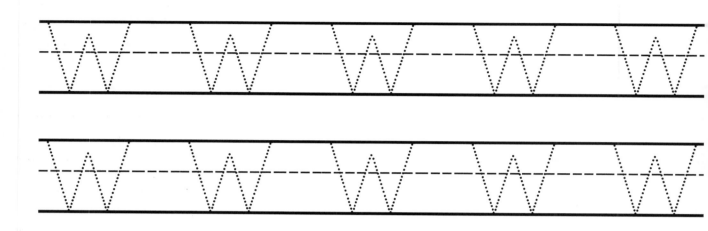

Trace the lowercase letters

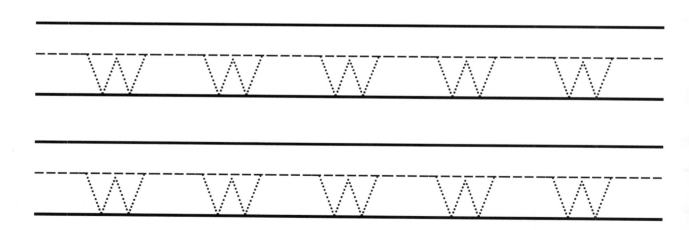

Ww

Trace the uppercase letters

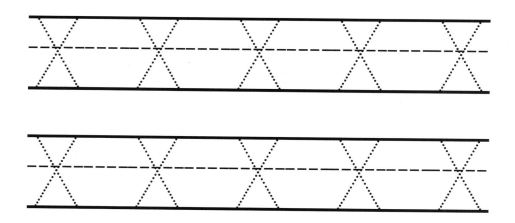

Trace the lowercase letters

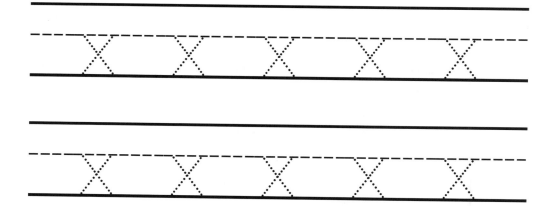

Xx

Trace the uppercase letters

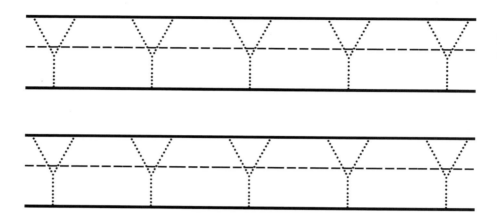

Trace the lowercase letters

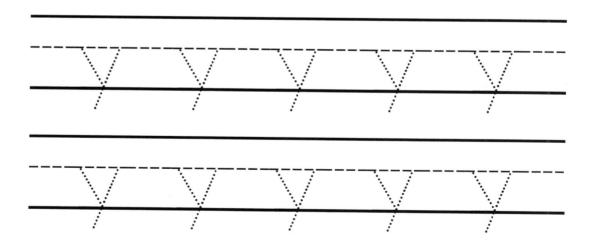

Yy

Trace the uppercase letters

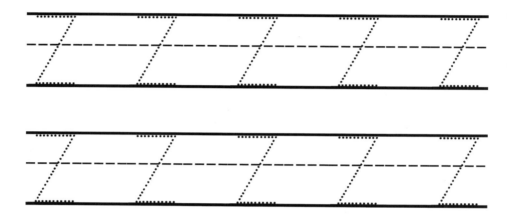

Trace the lowercase letters

Zz

CREATIVE SPACE

Siohan Scholars presents
this certificate to

for completion of the

Alphabet Handwriting
PRACTICE WORKBOOK

Made in the USA
Columbia, SC
29 March 2025